Two-in-One Series

Animal Tales From Africa

Illustrated by Johann Strauss

Fantasi • Pretoria

King Lion hands out gifts

Long, long ago the animals decided they wanted a king.
At a meeting they chose Lion. He was so pleased to be king
that he invited them all to a great feast that lasted for many
days.

 On the last day there was to be a dance. As Queen Lion
wanted all the animals to look their best, she begged her
husband to hand out gifts to all, so they would look smart.
"I'll do that," said Lion, "but if any animal annoys me or
didn't come to the feast, they're in trouble."

 He called all the animals to file
past him and tell him what gifts
they would like. First were
the cattle. "We'd like pretty
horns and lots of milk for
our calves," they asked.

"Fine," said Lion, "but as you prefer to live with Farmer rather than in my kingdom, I'll give only the bulls horns so that he can harness them.

To milk the cows he will just have to slip a rope round their necks. In that way your calves won't get all the milk." The cattle were satisfied, because they wanted to stay with Farmer.

Kudu arrived alone. "Where is your wife?" roared Lion. "My wife is very upset that she ignored our invitation. You want horns, do you? I'll give you these magnificent curved horns, but your wife gets nothing."

Elephant was next. He wanted a pair of white horns. Instead of waiting until Lion placed them on his head, he greedily picked them up in his mouth. This irritated Lion. "Now those horns will stay in your mouth as tusks," he growled.

Elephant, who at that time had a rather short snout, asked for a longer one. Lion, still cross, said, "All right, you want a long nose, you'll get one."

And Elephant's long trunk sank to the ground in front of him. Unhappy and sorry for himself, Elephant walked away, dragging his trunk in the dust.

Rhino came up, huffing and puffing. He pushed his thick upper lip into the presents. Lion was furious. "Can't you wait your turn? You will now have two heavy horns on your nose. Maybe that will teach you better manners!" The horns were so heavy that poor Rhino's nose dragged on the ground.

Hippo was even more high and mighty. She walked right in among the presents. "Hey, you!" roared Lion. "No horns for you. All you get are two huge teeth to defend yourself with." Hippo had to leave without horns.

Then it was Sheep's turn. Lion felt sorry for him, as he looked so miserable in his thin skin.

"I'll give you a warm, woolly coat," he said kindly, "but as you prefer to stay with Farmer, he may shear your wool once a year to make clothes for himself."

Billy Goat and Nanny Goat were next in line. They asked for sharp hooves, a beard for Billy and horns. The other animals were getting restless in the long queue.

As he was in a hurry, Lion gave Nanny Goat a beard as well. The other animals had a good laugh about this.

Snake approached on his short legs. He wanted to be a doctor, he said, and asked for all kinds of medicine. When Lion handed it to him, he drank it all up in one gulp. This made him run round in circles, trying to bite the others in the queue. "Quickly," shouted Lion, "cut off his legs!" Since then Snake has glided on his stomach.

Leguan, Snake and Lizard made such a racket arguing in the row, that Lion ordered that their tongues must be split in two. That's why they all have forked tongues.

Honey Badger and Skunk came to stand in front of Lion. "We'd like to smell good to impress the ladies tonight," they said. King Lion gave them some herbs to boil together for the perfume they wanted.

Those two were in such a hurry that they did not cook them long enough. The brew smelt awful, but they thought they smelled good and were most surprised when the other animals ran away when they came close.

Then it was Zebra's turn. "Oh, great King," he said, "my wife and I would like to pull your carriage."

"What a wonderful idea," said Lion, and he gave each of them a smart, striped suit.

Suddenly there was a lot of noise down the line where Porcupine was complaining loudly that they were pushing him out of the queue. "Don't worry, Porcupine," said

Lion, "I'll give you a suit of needle-sharp quills to wear. Nobody will push you again." Porcupine was delighted with his suit of long, quivering quills.

Rock Rabbit and Tortoise were last. Rock Rabbit was pleased with the sticky paws Lion gave her. With these paws he could climb the steepest krans.

When Tortoise complained about his short legs, Lion gave him four long legs so that he could see over the bushes. Unfortunately he couldn't balance on these long legs and the wind kept on blowing him over. He begged Lion to give back his short legs. Lion, roaring with laughter, agreed to do so. Since that day Tortoise has stayed mostly under bushy plants.

Everybody came to receive a gift, except frog. Where was he? Well, he went for a swim in the dam and naughty children hid his clothes. He was too shy to go to the feast without his clothes. To this day he swims around naked in the rivers and ponds.

Can you tell the story in your own words?

King Lion

Kudu and his horns

Hippopotamus

Zebra

Porcupine

Frog is naked

Baboon gets dressed in his Sunday best

One morning old Baboon sat on a large rock, basking in the sun. He was making a smart suit for himself to wear when he next visited his girlfriend. The last time he had seen her he had boasted about his fancy new clothes.

He draped a bushbuck skin around his shoulders as a cloak. He used a pair of ox hooves as boots, topped by two pieces of crinkly bark tied around his legs. He very carefully made a hat out of a bird's nest. Just as he was decorating it with a huge ostrich feather, he heard someone call out, "Hello, hello!"

It was Jackal who had crept up behind him. "My word, Monkey-face, what on earth are you doing? You look ridiculous."

Baboon had got a fright, but when he saw that it was only Jackal, King Lion's adviser, he smiled at him over his shoulder and said, "Go on, insult me as much as you like.

You'll eat your words when I go walking down the road to my girlfriend."

Jackal, always ready with his bag of tricks, said slyly, "You're right! In fact, my friend, you look wonderful. All you need now is a smart scarf and a pair of brown gloves."

"Really?" exclaimed Baboon, "but where will I get them?"

"Oh, that's no problem," replied Jackal. "Under that stone over there, you'll find a lovely scarf. And in that tree, there's the kind of gum that all the well-dressed people use to make gloves. There you go. What more do you want?"

With a broad smile Baboon jumped off the rock and swaggered to the large stone. As he lifted the stone he saw a blue and red-striped scarf, a garter snake!

The snake was stiff from the cold. With a pleased smile Baboon draped the snake around his neck. He then walked to the gum tree where he smeared a thick layer of gum on his hands. Now he had everything he needed.

Back on the rock, he waited for the gum to dry. But, oh dear, the gum got so hard that Baboon couldn't move his fingers. In the meantime the snake, getting warmer and warmer, was wrapping itself tighter and tighter around Baboon's neck.

"Stop that!" shouted Baboon,
but he couldn't use his stiff
fingers to get rid of the snake.
The snake coiled even tighter.
"Aarggh!" choked
Baboon, twisting this
way and that, turning
somersaults in the dust.
His eyes bulged and he
bared his teeth, trying
to speak. No sound.
Poor old Baboon!
What should he do
now?

The waterhole! Splash! He dived deeply, but the snake clung even tighter. Baboon was fighting for his life.

At last the snake stiffened in the cold water and let go. Out of breath, Baboon struggled to the edge of the waterhole and crawled out.

Naked and wet, he gasped out insults at Jackal for getting him into this mess. "You lying, two-faced scumbag! I'll get you back for this!"

Jackal, of course, was helpless with laughter. Yes, with all this wrestling in the water, Baboon had lost his clothes. He did not really mind: he had had enough of clothes.

As a matter of fact, if you try and dress up a baboon today, he'll tear the clothes off his body.
At last Baboon walked to his girlfriend who had been waiting impatiently for him to arrive in his Sunday best.

She was surprised when he arrived without any clothes. "And where are those fine, new clothes you told me about?" she wanted to know.

When he told her the story, she laughed and made fun of him. Ashamed, he slunk away with his tail between his legs and quietly joined his own troop. Since then baboons have always driven away strange baboons from their group. They know that if they don't, the strangers will always remind them of this embarrassing story.